The Dreams of Hummingbirds
Poems from Nature

Mary Ann Coleman

Illustrated by Robert Masheris

ALBERT WHITMAN & COMPANY ◆ Morton Grove, Illinois

For Sarah and Sean
and for all
who truly treasure our world.
M.A.C.

The illustrations are watercolors.
The text typeface is Leawood.
Book designed by Robert Masheris.

Text © 1993 by Mary Ann Coleman.
Illustrations © 1993 by Robert Masheris.
Published in 1993 by Albert Whitman & Company,
6340 Oakton Street, Morton Grove, Illinois 60053.
Published simultaneously in Canada
by General Publishing, Limited, Toronto.

Library of Congress Cataloging-in-Publication Data
Coleman, Mary Ann.
The dreams of hummingbirds: poems from nature /
Mary Ann Coleman; illustrated by Robert Masheris.
p. cm.
Summary: Eighteen poems of nature and ecology.
ISBN 0-8075-1720-8
1. Nature—Juvenile poetry. [1. Nature—Poetry.
2. American poetry.] I. Masheris, Robert, ill.
II. Title.
PS3553.04744D7 1993   92-28169
811'.54—dc20   CIP
                                   AC

Whenever I was outdoors as a child, I felt free. I was never lonely, even when I was alone, for nature spoke to me with bird cry and leaf rustle. The sky was a dazzle of blue; the wind brushing against my face was a friend's warm touch. The changing shapes of clouds formed my own moving pictures in the sky. And there were nights when I drifted to sleep to the soft tick-tack of rain drumming on our roof.

Yet I often took these gifts for granted.

Because forces have been set in motion that have depleted our natural resources, it's time for us to become caretakers of the earth. We must never think one person can't make a difference—often people have single-handedly changed the world.

Still, you will not be alone. Many are working to rescue our planet. Now, you could be a volunteer in a nature center or help with recycling. Later, you might choose a career as an inventor or work in conservation research. There are many pathways you can find to help preserve the wonder of our world.

One summer evening in the mountains, I saw a crowd of fireflies above a lawn, each one streaking upward in the darkness. A single light magnified a hundredfold became a glorious and moving sight. This vision gave me courage, made me aware of the force that we possess. Our individual efforts, too, can unite to kindle fires in the minds of others.

Our earth can be changed for the better. You have the power to create that change.

Bicycle Trip

A poem
is like an
unplanned
trip by bicycle.
The wind of words
blows in your ears.
Jack-in-the-Pulpits,
Lady Slippers
become the handlebars.
You begin to understand
fireplugs shining in the sun,
the wild toss of bachelor buttons.

The limits of the street change, shrink—
two-lane highways, a country road.
Then with an unexpected lurch,
thought turns into a side dirt path
where stones and pine straw lie
and hickories grow, shaggy and gray.
A lake opens, a mountain roars.
Surprised, you're part of the landscape.

The Beat of Spring

It starts slowly
when you're asleep.
Roots flicker
like the tongues
of tiny snakes.

Then the beat quickens.

Tender shoots
push up toward the sun,
reach toward birth.

Now the tempo
is louder still
as the boom
      boom
    boom
of
creation
rocks
the
earth.

*L*izard

Lizard climbing
on my roof,
your tail disappearing
beyond the eaves
as you skitter across
the shingles—
please
don't rush
away.

I won't harm you.

Come,
sunbathe
in our garden,
warm your stomach
on our rocks.

Our mosses can be your bed.

For breakfast
I'll bring you
delicious flies.
And dead gnats
to use
for pepper.

Let's
live in
harmony
together.

*T*he Lake

Rowing
past the calls
of parents on shore,
I push the boat far
beyond docks and pines
creaking in high wind
like rocking chairs.

I row
to the lake's center
where I sing
and talk to the world.
There's nobody to know.
The sun is warm
on my back, my neck.
The waves, twisting by,
slow for me.

And free, I rule
the whispering waters,
the rushing
sweep of crows,
the deep,
cloud-feathered
sky.

If I Were a Hawk

If I were a hawk,
I would taste the tips of storm clouds
and clutch lightning bolts in my great claws.
I'd fold my wings and dive into forests
green as the Atlantic
with the wind polishing my feathers,
and then flap away again.

I'd fly through a hundred cloud-patched sunsets,
and hammer sungold to the pines with my curved beak.
I'd name the whole sky mine and call aloud to claim it,
circling the world till night eased me down on my nest.
An umbrella of stars over my shoulders,
I'd sleep without fear or nightmare in the dark
if I were a hawk.

Alaskan Summer

Now days linger into the night.
Winds still blow cool.
Huge wildflowers
stir on every hill.

Seagulls coast and wheel
where our fishing boats go.
Gull feathers swirling in the air—
Alaska's summer snow.

hickets

The sun
rehearses its rising
once more.
                Still
there are places where the light
is dim. Thickets where rabbits
munch grasses. And ants
erect cathedrals to their gods.
                        Pines wear sculptures
of lichen on their limbs . . . and there
you'll find a pond where algae puddles,
where lily pads float and ripple
with the small weight of dragonflies.

Toward evening a mockingbird cries
Praise for all this green.

*T*he Dolphin

glides through the glass
green waters of the Seaquarium,
remembering the deep calls
of whales,
the way he rolled
in great blue passages
of open sea
thinking out loud.
Song-thought.
Shrill notes as he rose
through plankton and sea-weed,
gleams of the sun that drifted
      down
         down
covering his skin
with golden nets.

Evening. He lifts
from the tank,
jumping free.
Sees the moon
splintering its silver
against the waves.

Afterward his clicks,
chitters, whistles
become a longing,
his speech a song
that includes the moon,
its glitter in an ocean
blue as the long-ago sea
calling inside him.

Listening,
he waits for an answer.

Saguaro Cactus

A four-story
apartment building;
woodpeckers,
your construction crew,
peck openings.

Soon the elf owl,
five inches tall,
looks out of your
superstructure.
Then tiny baby owls
appear,
cry for insects
and scorpions
in their cactus home.

When all have flown,
your spiny needles dropped,
your outer shell of fleshy green
eaten by birds and animals—
your inner wooden form,
cross-shaped,
blown
by desert
winds,
remains.

Desert Evening

Late afternoon.
Thick orange clouds
hang above. The landscape
darkens. Trees shiver
in a sudden wind.

                Thunderclaps.
Lightning rakes across the sky
like a witch's sharp fingernails.

Magically, torrents
of rain turn the air to silver.
Presto! Trees and shrubs
become invisible.
Celebrating,
spadefoot toads call out.

Millipedes move from under rocks,
strange rippling trains crossing
the desert sand.
             And the sky
clears.

Overhead, the evening
star appears.

Return Favor

The blue
boulevard of the sky,
the blue
onion dome of the sky,
the blue
upside-down
cradle of the sky—
whatever costume it wears,
beneath it I run, I live, I play.

As a return favor,
I'll be a caretaker under the
robin's egg blue of the sky.

I know there are other colors
drifting in the air,
colors the human eye can't see,
but the blue sail of the sky
unfurling every day
is fine enough for me.

Deer in Snow

At the end
of a snow-powdered
tunnel of leaves,
two deer
eat the tender bark
of trees
in early winter.

As the doe
moves forward,
small twigs
crack
under her hooves.

The buck
pushes gently on
as veils of snow
fall from a hemlock.

Why is it one feels
an unspoken prayer
in the eyes of deer?

Those two tourists
traveling together,
buck and doe,
buck
and
delicate
doe.

Sea Poems

The Tide

Waves strike the shore
with the whoosh
of a fire-eater's flaming breath.

Clam

I don't blame you
for flexing your muscle tight—
all that sweet fluid
to bathe in,
not one faucet to turn.

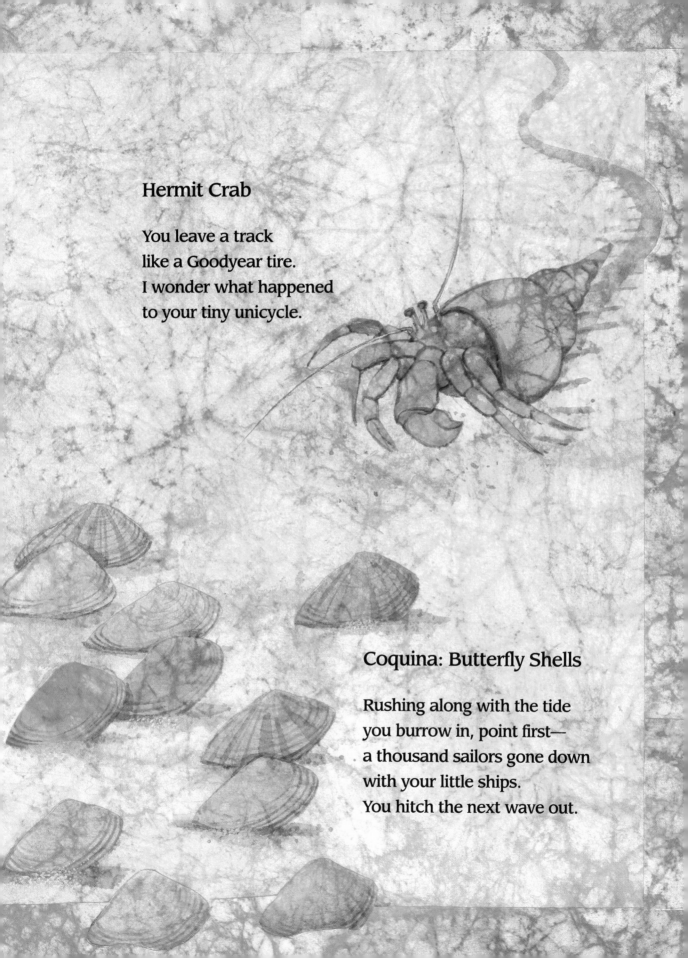

Hermit Crab

You leave a track
like a Goodyear tire.
I wonder what happened
to your tiny unicycle.

Coquina: Butterfly Shells

Rushing along with the tide
you burrow in, point first—
a thousand sailors gone down
with your little ships.
You hitch the next wave out.

The Bass

The bass hides in dusty weeds,
weeds like brown feathers stuck in mud,
shed from some monstrous bird.

In his cool world
of algaed roots and stones,
his fins fan, delicate
as an onion's skin.
                    He darts
through the lake's small tides
into tall, waving grasses
and rests a moment.
Then
        he darts
                again
to oversee his vast
and shadowy kingdom.

On Meeting a Turtle by a Gravel Road

Turtle
stopped by the road,
as I lift you,
you
   gaze
     steadily
at me, then slow-
  ly,
    slow-ly,
  softer
   than
    a sigh
you hinge yourself shut,
     a hermit
giving up on the world.

If I, dependent on this earth, this sky
could read those messages
you wear scratched on your shell
and your mysterious signs—
patterns
of yellow & deepest
chocolate brown
flung how many eons ago
from a burning star . . .

In the meantime, I'll find some moss
and put you gently down.

*F*light: The Albatross

Full moon and the tide
high. Wind rush
and the great bird
lifts above the waves,
glides beyond the coast.

      Moonward he sails,
ghost-white, his wings spread
but still.

      Above him,
the North Star shines, Pegasus,
Andromeda. And below, star prints
on the sea.

      He veers,
tilts with the wind, navigates
a course his body knows.

Days when cloud-shadows
on the water slide
with the shadow of his wings,
pacing his long voyage.

And the night again, flying
with the updrafts, the moon
growing smaller, a crescent finally.

Many nights and days as he flies
between layers of stars and moon,
between the sky's ocean of sunlight
and the real sea, ever gliding,
mute on motionless wings, sailing
till the trip is done,
flying down,
down to the shore,
still wild in this shining world.

The Nest

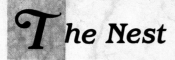

Her day's just begun—
the ruby-throated hummingbird
drinks from the blue funnel
of the morning glory.
Then, from her dream
she builds;
her nest
a spider's
abandoned web,
emerald green mosses,
pale blue-green lichen,
mud,
leafmold—
offerings
from the living world.

Spirits of ancestors
hover nearby,
spirits that speak from the dream,
guiding her, showing the way.

With movements more rapid
than the human heart can beat,
she makes a cup
for the flurry
of other wings,
for the cool,
quicksilver
light
each blessed
morning
brings.

Lifting a Strawberry from a Bowl of Fruit

Strawberries—
worlds the color of Mars.
I slice one across
and in its pale center
a planet explodes.
Rays of the blast
stretch out
like the beams of the sun.

I lift another strawberry
from the bowl.
Gnats, small moons,
circle it
while I,
ruler of the universe,
hold a world
in the palm of my hand.